When I Was Young

and

WiLD BiLL'S SECRET WiSH

LEARNING
MEDIA®

Distributed in the United States of America by Pacific Learning,
P.O. Box 2723, Huntington Beach, CA 92647-0723
Web site: www.pacificlearning.com

Published 1999 by Learning Media Limited,
Box 3293, Wellington 6001, New Zealand
Web site: www.learningmedia.com

10 9 8 7 6 5 4 3

Printed in Hong Kong

ISBN 0 478 22941 0

PL 9166

CONTENTS

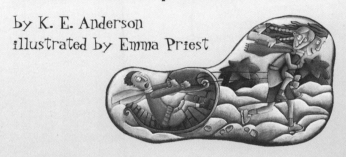

When I Was Young

by K.E. Anderson

Dear Uncle Phillip

I'm doing a project at school about how
times have changed over the last fifty
years. I have been talking to Mom about
what it was like when she went to school.
   Is it true that Mom had to walk for
three hours in bare feet through snow and
over mountains and through raging rivers
just to get to school?

Love from Karen

Dear Karen

I think your mother's memory is playing tricks on her. As you know, she is my little sister, and she hated walking in those days. So … I had to piggyback her through the snow and over the mountains and through the raging rivers. In fact, I had to piggyback my other sister, Raewyn, as well. And I had to sing them songs to keep them amused.

A friend always came along with us, but she kept on getting lost along the way, and I'd have to go back to look for her. That took up quite a bit of time, I can tell you!

I hope this helps with your project. And, by the way, it took us five hours to get to school, not three.

Love from Uncle Phillip

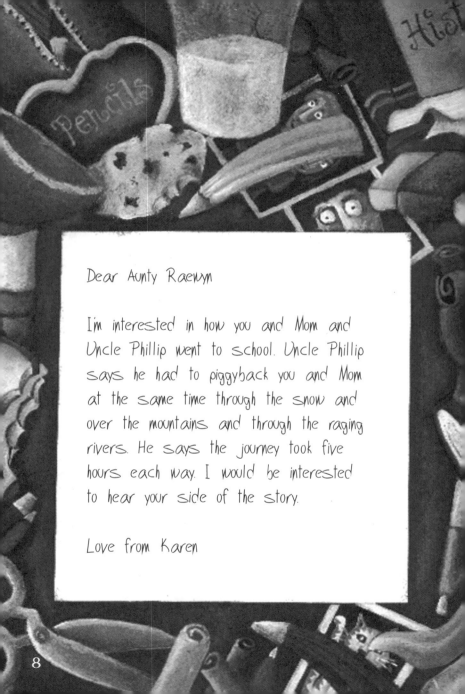

Dear Aunty Raewyn

I'm interested in how you and Mom and Uncle Phillip went to school. Uncle Phillip says he had to piggyback you and Mom at the same time through the snow and over the mountains and through the raging rivers. He says the journey took five hours each way. I would be interested to hear your side of the story.

Love from Karen

Dear Karen

I love my brother dearly, but I think he must have a disease which affects his memory. I was the one who had to do all the carrying! Your Uncle Phillip used to sit in a sled I made him when he got too big to piggy-back. With your mother on my back, and the sled rope tied around my waist, I'd make the journey through the snow, over the mountains, and through raging rivers in just over six hours.

Let me know how you get on with your project.

Love
Aunty Raewyn

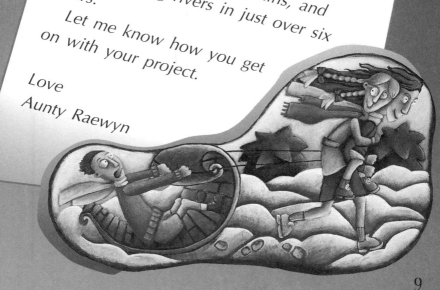

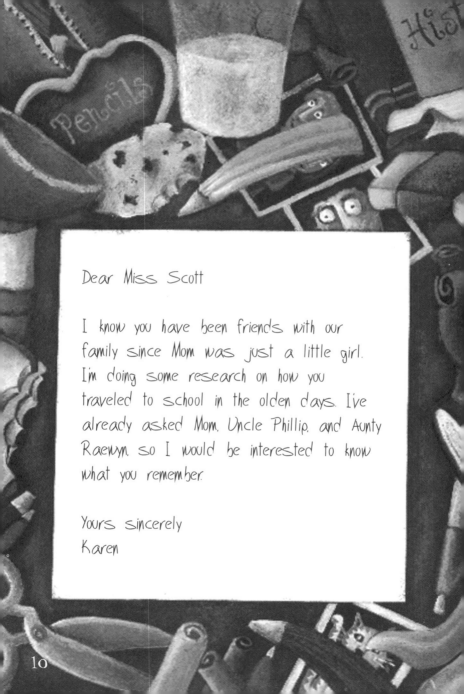

Dear Miss Scott

I know you have been friends with our family since Mom was just a little girl. I'm doing some research on how you traveled to school in the olden days. I've already asked Mom, Uncle Phillip, and Aunty Raewyn, so I would be interested to know what you remember.

Yours sincerely
Karen

Dear Karen

Firstly, how is your Uncle Phillip?
I haven't heard from him for such a long time.
Is he married yet? I bet he looks as handsome
as ever.

You probably don't realize it, but I'm
the oldest of us all (only just, mind you).
Because I'm the oldest, I had to push your
mother and aunty and uncle to school in a
wheelbarrow. The journey through snow
and over mountains and through raging
rivers took about eight hours. And I had no
shoes and only a dry crust for breakfast!

Say "hello" to Phillip for me.
It was lovely to hear from you.

Yours sincerely
Janet Scott

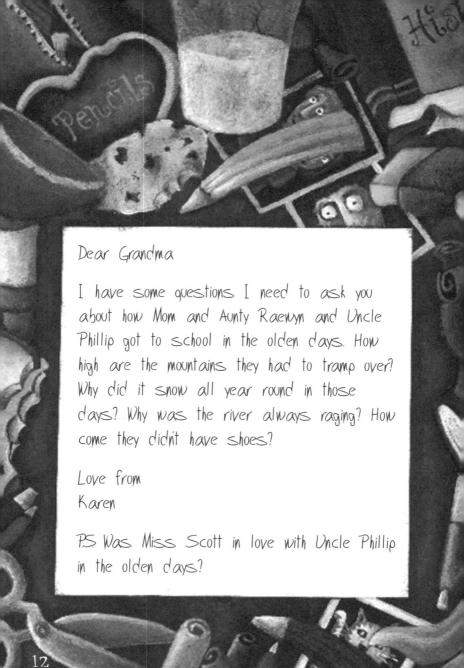

Dear Grandma

I have some questions I need to ask you about how Mom and Aunty Raewyn and Uncle Phillip got to school in the olden days. How high are the mountains they had to tramp over? Why did it snow all year round in those days? Why was the river always raging? How come they didn't have shoes?

Love from
Karen

P.S. Was Miss Scott in love with Uncle Phillip in the olden days?

Dear Karen

How lovely to hear from you. I think Janet Scott and your uncle were too busy doing schoolwork to be falling in love. How interesting that they are both not married. I am thinking of having a dinner party. Could you send me Janet Scott's address. What night does your uncle play baseball? I need to know so I don't make the dinner party on that night.

Honestly! I think your mother and aunty and uncle have all got serious problems. Very serious problems indeed. Especially when it comes to their memories!

They actually caught the school bus to school every day. All they had to do was walk down the farm track to the road, which took them about two minutes. The ride into town took twenty minutes on the bus.

13

Now, if you really want to know about hard times, I can tell you all about it! When I was a girl, I had to get up in the middle of the night and milk the cows, feed the hens, clean the house, cook the breakfast for the farmhands, make lunch, and feed and change my little sister, Wendy. Then I had to walk for ten hours through mud and snow and hail, battling terrible winds and freezing temperatures all the way. I had no shoes or jacket or hat. The mountains in those days were much higher than they are now, and the raging rivers were so deep and wide, I became an expert swimmer and was chosen for the Olympic swimming team. I hope this helps with your schoolwork.

Love from
Grandma

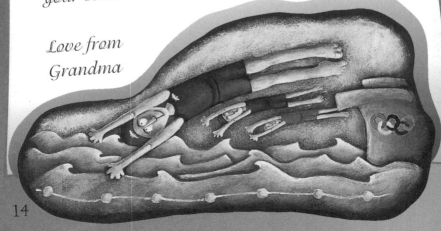

Dear Great-aunty Wendy

Grandma said ...

illustrated by Emma Priest

WILD BILL'S SECRET WISH

by Brian Birchall

Wild Bill Miggs went out into the garden and hid behind a shrub. He held his breath and crossed his fingers and said "Ping-pong" three times with his eyes closed.

When he heard Penny the Postal Worker's footsteps on the path outside, and when he heard a "flop" as the mail dropped into his letter box, he knew it had worked. Wild Bill Miggs smiled quietly and kept still ….

Then Penny went off down the street. Wild Bill Miggs opened his eyes, stepped quietly out from behind the shrub, and skipped around in a big circle on the lawn. He looked up at Blackbird sitting on the telephone wires and smiled as he walked up to his mailbox and took out the mail.

One long brown envelope with a window and …

W. B. Miggs
10 Seagull Street
Penguin Bay

… peeping out at him. "Bah!" said Wild Bill Miggs. "It's printed! It's a bill! Bah!"

One long white envelope with …

To the Occupant

… printed on the front. "Rats!" said Wild Bill Miggs, looking up at Blackbird sitting on the telephone wire. "That's not just for me – everybody got one of them!"

There was a piece of floppy yellow paper saying that there would be a meeting of the Penguin Club next Thursday, and a sheet of paper with colored pictures of plants for the garden. "Bah! Rats and bats!" said Wild Bill Miggs. "Who wants plants? This garden's full of them!"

A shiny book with colored pictures of smiling women wearing new clothes. "No! No!" said Wild Bill Miggs. "Why do they keep sending me books selling women's clothes?"

A long green envelope with a window and ...

W. B. Miggs
10 Seagull Street
Penguin Bay

"Bah! Another bill! Rats and bats and buzzing bees!" shouted Wild Bill Miggs. And that was all there was in the box! No letters for him with real wobbly writing on them, like ...

Mr. Wild Bill Miggs
10 Seagull Street
Penguin Bay

No real letters that were written by human beings with their own human hands!

Wild Bill Miggs threw down the mail – window letters, the book about women's clothes, the paper with pictures of garden plants, and the Penguin Club notice. He threw them all down on the grass and jumped on them.

"This always happens ... every day!" Wild Bill Miggs shouted up at Blackbird. "I get all this mail, but none of it's really for me ... Wild Bill Miggs!"

21

Blackbird put its head on one side and looked down at Wild Bill Miggs through one orange eye.

"I wait for the mail every morning … I hide behind the shrub … I cross my fingers and close my eyes and say 'Ping-pong' three times – and that's all I get!" Wild Bill Miggs pointed at the mail lying on the grass.

Blackbird put up its head and started a whistling song.

"And you keep quiet!" Wild Bill Miggs shouted up at the blackbird. "I don't feed you crumbs every morning to be laughed at!"

Blackbird stopped the whistling song and looked down at Wild Bill Miggs.

"And wipe that smile off your beak!" Wild Bill shouted as he jumped up and down on his mail. He jumped and stamped and kicked and shouted: "Bah … bah! Junk and bills! Rats! … Bats! And buzz …"

He was just going to shout "Buzzing bees" when a voice from over the front fence said: "Why, Mr. Miggs! What *are* you doing?"

Wild Bill stopped jumping and shouting and looked around. It was the Postal Worker.

"Oh!" said Wild Bill, scratching his nose. "Oh, hello, Penny … I was er … er … er … just … jumping on my mail. And … er … er … telling Blackbird to keep quiet!"

"Why do you want to do things like that?" asked Penny.

"Well," said Wild Bill. "Well, I look forward to you bringing me the mail … but I'm sick of only getting letters from computers. These computers only want me to send them money or want me to buy things I don't need …. They don't know me … they don't want to know me! They just want me to do things for them. I'm sick of it!"

"What kind of letters would you like, Mr. Wild Bill?" asked Penny. "I might be able to help you if I know."

"I want letters from people I know. I want letters from my old friends and my family. I want letters asking about how I am and what I'm doing. I want letters with my name and address written on the front in real wobbly writing."

"Well, that's easy!" said Penny. "All you have to do is to write letters to all your old friends and family and ask them what they are doing and how they are. Ask them if they're getting boring letters from computers ... and if they have a blackbird to feed. They'll write back to you, and I'll bring you their letters each morning."

"That's a great idea!" said Wild Bill Miggs. "That's great! I never thought of that! I'll go inside and start right away. What a good idea! Thank you, Penny."

And Wild Bill Miggs picked up all his muddy, trampled mail and went inside to find a pen and paper.

Penny walked back up Seagull Street carrying her bag of mail.

Wild Bill Miggs started his first letter:

10 Seagull Street
Penguin Bay

May 10

Dear Cousin Kate
I was just wondering how you and Tim
and the family and the canary are getting on.
What was the canary's name – Poppy,
wasn't it? . . .

10 Seagull Street
Penguin Bay

May 10

Dear Johnny Black
I was just wondering how you and Mrs.
Black and the family are getting on. Do you
ever come down near Penguin Bay? ...

10 Seagull Street
Penguin Bay

May 10

Dear Benny
I was just thinking the other day about when
we were at school together. How are you
getting on now? Do you remember that funny
teacher we had with the big ears? .... Do you
still go on vacation to Toronto? How is your
dog, Tomkin? And do you still go shopping
with Tomkin pulling you along on that
old red bicycle? ...

Wild Bill put stamps on the letters and posted them at the Penguin Bay Post Office.

Soon, he started to get real letters! Real, friendly letters with Wild Bill's name and address written on the front in wobbly writing. They were letters written by people that he knew! Letters written by human beings instead of computers!

One day, Wild Bill Miggs waited
beside his letter box – he didn't hide
from Penny the Postal Worker any more.
When she handed Wild Bill his mail, he
gave her a letter back.

"Don't open it until you get home!"
said Wild Bill Miggs.

When Penny got home and opened
the letter, this what it said:

10 Seagull Street
Penguin Bay

July 8

Dear Penny
Thank you for helping me to find all my old
friends and relatives! As you know, now I get
lots of mail from real people . . . human beings
who write in wobbly handwriting.
It's great.

Your friend
Wild Bill Miggs

illustrated by Philip Webb